Bunny Riddles

Katy Hall and Lisa Eisenberg
pictures by Nicole Rubel

Dial Books for Young Readers

 New York

Published by Dial Books for Young Readers
A member of Penguin Putnam Inc.
375 Hudson Street
New York, New York 10014

The Dial Easy-to-Read logo is a registered trademark of
Dial Books for Young Readers,
a division of Penguin Books USA Inc.,
® TM 1,162,718.

Library of Congress Cataloging in Publication Data
Hall, Katy. Bunny riddles /
by Katy Hall and Lisa Eisenberg ; pictures by Nicole Rubel.
p.   cm.
Summary: Forty-two riddles about rabbits.
Example: Do bunnies use combs? No, they use hare brushes.
ISBN 0-8037-1519-6—ISBN 0-8037-1521-8 (library)
1. Riddles, Juvenile. 2. Rabbits—Juvenile humor.
[1. Rabbits—Wit and humor. 2. Riddles. 3. Jokes.]
I. Eisenberg, Lisa. II. Rubel, Nicole, ill. III. Title.
PN6371.5.H3474 1997 818'.5402—dc20 93-13241 CIP AC

First Edition
3 5 7 9 10 8 6 4 2

*The paintings, which consist of black ink and colored markers,
are color-separated and reproduced in full color.*

Reading Level 2.4

What happened when the
magician did a scary trick?

His hare stood on end!

What do little bunnies sing
at birthday parties?

"Hoppy birthday to you!"

What's the difference
between an angry rabbit
and a phony dollar bill?

One is a mad bunny and
the other is some bad money!

What did the rabbits say
when the farmer caught
them kissing in the garden?

"Lettuce alone!"

What did the rabbit give his girlfriend when he asked her to marry him?

A 14-carrot ring!

Where did the rabbits go after they got married?

On their bunnymoon!

Do bunnies use combs?

No, they use hare brushes!

Why did the little girl
wash her rabbit?

Because her hare was dirty!

What do you call a bunny
that likes to play
hide-and-seek with foxes?

Dinner!

What do you call a carrot
that insults a rabbit?

A fresh vegetable!

What would you get if
you crossed a terrier with
a rabbit?

A hare-dale!

Where did the famous
flyer Amelia Harehart like
to land her plane?

At O'Hare International Hareport!

Why did the bunnies go
on strike?

They wanted a raise in celery!

Where do Easter bunnies go
to dance?

To the Basket Ball!

Who catches bank robber
bunnies?

Agents of the F.B.I.—
Federal *Burrow* of Investigation!

How do bunnies get
from one vegetable garden
to another?

They take a taxi cabbage!

Where do rich snowshoe
rabbits keep all their money?

In the snow bank!

What do you call a bunny
that's stuck in the mud?

Unhoppy!

What happened to
the silly bunny who
put butter on his head?

Everything slipped his mind!

Why did the bald man put
a bunny on his head?

He wanted a full head of hare!

How did the rabbit
become a pilot?

He joined the Hare Force!

Why do snowshoe rabbits
see so well?

They have good ice sight!

How is a hairy bunny
like a long car trip?

It's fur from one end to the other!

What's the best way
to raise rabbits?

Pick them up!

What do rabbits say
when they drink a toast?

"Ears looking at you, kid!"

Why do all bunnies want
to be like snowshoe rabbits?

Because snowshoe rabbits are so cool!

What did Mr. and Mrs. Bunny
name their new baby girl?

Jenni-fur!

What is a *twip*?

What a wabbit takes
when it wides on a twain!

How can you catch a rabbit?

Hide under a bush and
make a noise like a carrot!

What dance do little rabbits
like to do?

The bunny hop!

Why was the bunny's nose
so shiny?

Its powder puff was on the wrong end!

What do you call a bunny with oodles of money?

A billion-hare!

Why did the rabbit build
herself a house?

She was fed up
with the *hole* thing!

What game do little bunnies like to play?

Hopscotch!

How did the hairy hare
help out at the wedding?

He was the beast man!

Why did the fox leave its den?

He wanted some fresh hare!

42

Which bunnies are wearing
Band-Aids?

The ones that just got harecuts!

What would you get if you
crossed a bunny with a giant?

A tall tail!

Why did the bunny take
a bottle of salad dressing
to bed with him?

So he'd be sure to get up oily!

Why did the tired bunnies stop playing basketball?

They were out of bounds!

What kind of bunny climbed the beanstalk?

A Jack rabbit!

What part of a book is like the back of a bunny?

This part—it's the tail end!